SPENCE

Based on *The Railway Series* by th

Illustrations by
Robin Davies and Jerry Smith

EGMONT

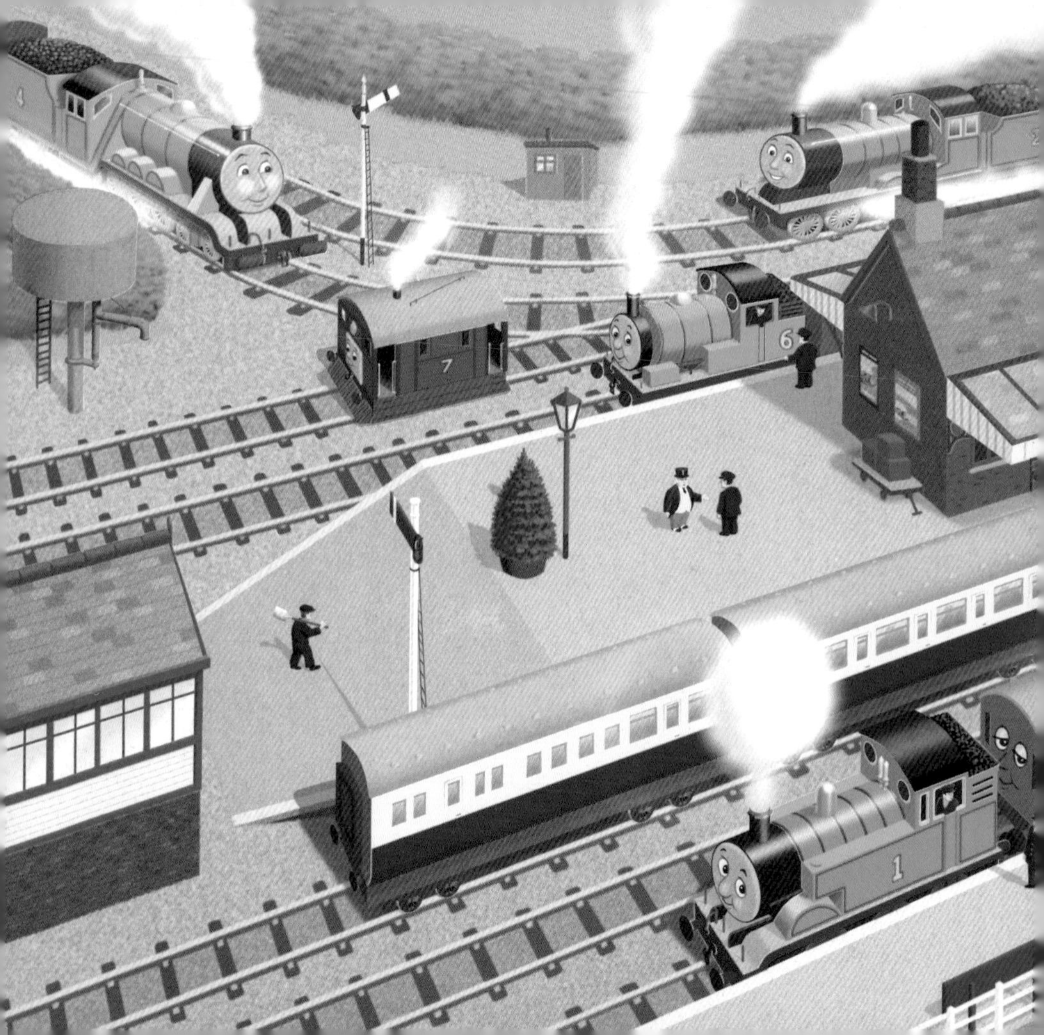

3
5

EGMONT

We bring stories to life

First published in Great Britain 2005
by Egmont UK Limited
239 Kensington High Street, London W8 6SA

Thomas the Tank Engine & Friends™

A BRITT ALLCROFT COMPANY PRODUCTION

Based on The Railway Series by The Reverend W Awdry

ISBN 978 1 4052 1721 7
5 7 9 10 8 6 4
Printed in Great Britain

TO THE TRAINS →

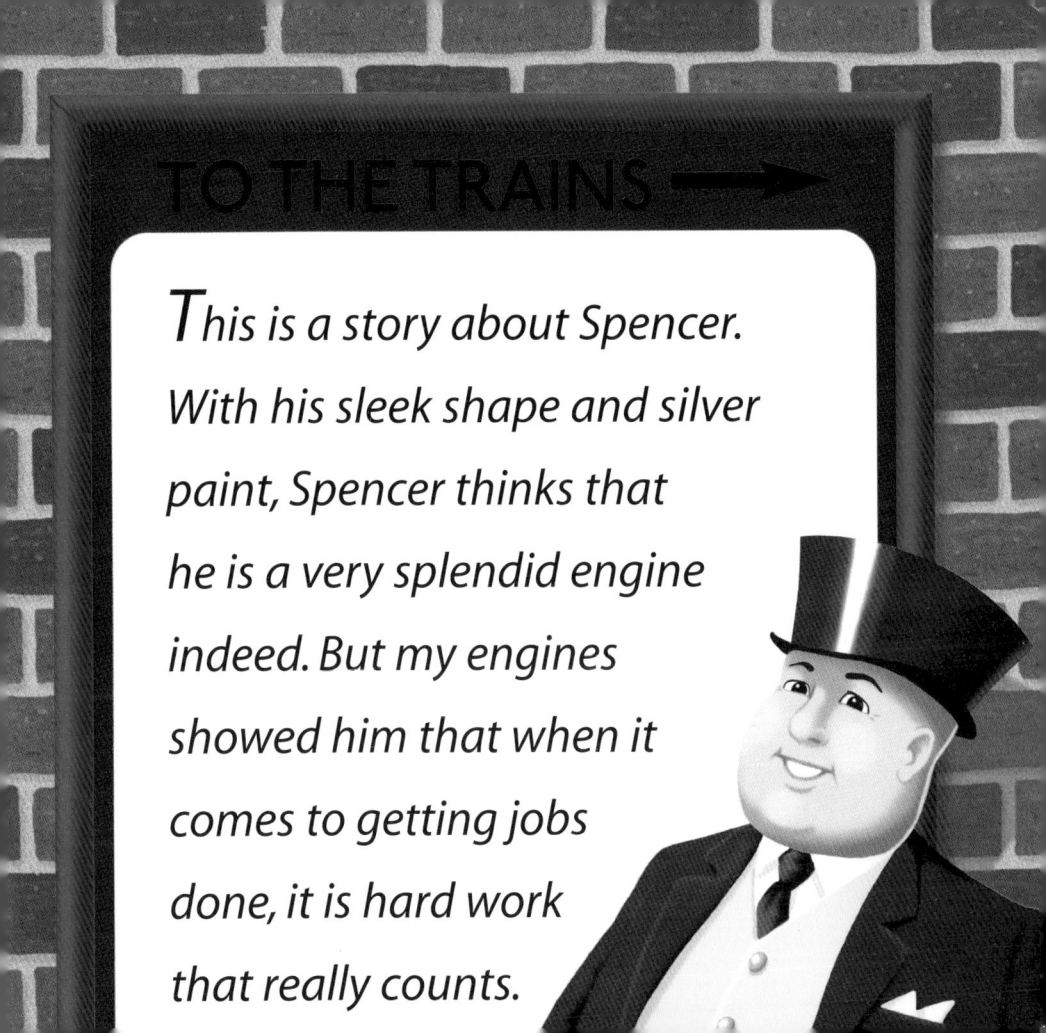

This is a story about Spencer. With his sleek shape and silver paint, Spencer thinks that he is a very splendid engine indeed. But my engines showed him that when it comes to getting jobs done, it is hard work that really counts.

One day, the Duke and Duchess came to Sodor for a visit. Gordon hoped that he would have the special job of showing the important visitors around the Island.

But, to Gordon's disappointment, the Duke and Duchess brought their own engine with them. His name was Spencer, and he was the shiniest, sleekest engine that Gordon had ever seen.

SPENCER

That afternoon, there was to be a party at Maron Station for the Duke and Duchess.

"That's on the other side of Gordon's Hill," James told Spencer.

"You'll need to take on plenty of water," Gordon added, helpfully.

"I have plenty of water," wheeshed Spencer, as he steamed out of the yard.

But when Spencer reached Gordon's Hill, he began to struggle. The hill was long and steep. He puffed. He panted. He pulled with all his might. But Spencer had run out of steam.

His Driver had to phone for help.

Back at the station, the Station Master told Gordon "The Fat Controller has a job for you. There's an engine stuck on a hill."

Gordon set off at once.

SPENCER

Gordon was surprised to find Spencer.

"What's wrong?" he asked.

"No water!" snapped Spencer. "I must have a leaky tank."

"Perhaps," smiled Gordon. "But we'd better hurry. Everyone is waiting for the Duke and Duchess."

Soon, Gordon was coupled up to Spencer, and they set off.

SPENCER

Minutes later, they arrived at Maron Station. The party was ready to begin.

"Well done, Gordon," said The Fat Controller. "You are a Very Useful Engine!"

Gordon glowed with pride.

MARON

Spencer was a very fast engine. One day, when he pulled into Knapford Station, his Driver had exciting news for him.

"You have beaten Gordon's record," he said.

"Of course," boasted Spencer. "I'm faster and finer than all the engines on Sodor put together."

The Fat Controller's engines were very cross.

3
4
SPENCER

Spencer was taking the Duke and Duchess to their summer house. The Fat Controller came to tell his engines that one of them was needed to carry their furniture. The engines saw the chance for a race!

"Please, Sir!" said Thomas, James and Gordon all together. "May I go?"

But The Fat Controller told Edward to go instead.

James and Gordon groaned. Edward was an old engine, and not as strong and fast as the others.

"He'll lose the race and let the whole Railway down!" said James.

Thomas and Percy were cross with James. Edward was their friend.

"You can beat that big, silver show-off any day!" they told him.

Slowly and steadily, Edward set off.

"Will-do-my-best, will-do-my-best," he puffed.

But Spencer quickly passed Edward.

"I've won already," he boasted.

And with a whoosh, he was gone!

SPENCER
2

Edward came to the bottom of a steep hill. The furniture was heavy and he felt tired.

But Donald and Douglas were waiting at the junction. They had heard about the race.

"Hoorah for Edward!" cried Donald.

"He's a first rate engine!" added Douglas.

This made Edward feel much better. He huffed and puffed and soon he had climbed to the top of the hill. He raced down the other side to catch up with Spencer.

Spencer happily steamed along. Up ahead was the siding leading to the summer house.

But the Duke wanted to take some photographs of the countryside. Spencer stopped, and the Duke set up his camera.

Spencer closed his eyes. "Nothing to worry about," he said, lazily.

Before long, Spencer was fast asleep.

When the Duke had finished taking photographs Spencer's Driver rang the bell.

"Time to go," he said.

Nothing happened.

Spencer was dreaming of winning the race. He didn't hear the bell. And he didn't hear Edward puffing past him. Spencer's Driver rang the bell again and again.

Finally, Spencer opened his eyes. He couldn't believe what he saw. Edward was heading towards the summer house.

"Nearly-there-nearly-there," gasped the old engine.

SPENCER

Spencer took off as fast as he could, but he was too late.

Edward pulled to a stop in front of the summer house.

“I’ve won,” he gasped. “I did it!”

Suddenly his pistons didn’t ache and his axles weren’t shaking. Edward felt like the pride of the Sodor Railway.

And he was right.

2

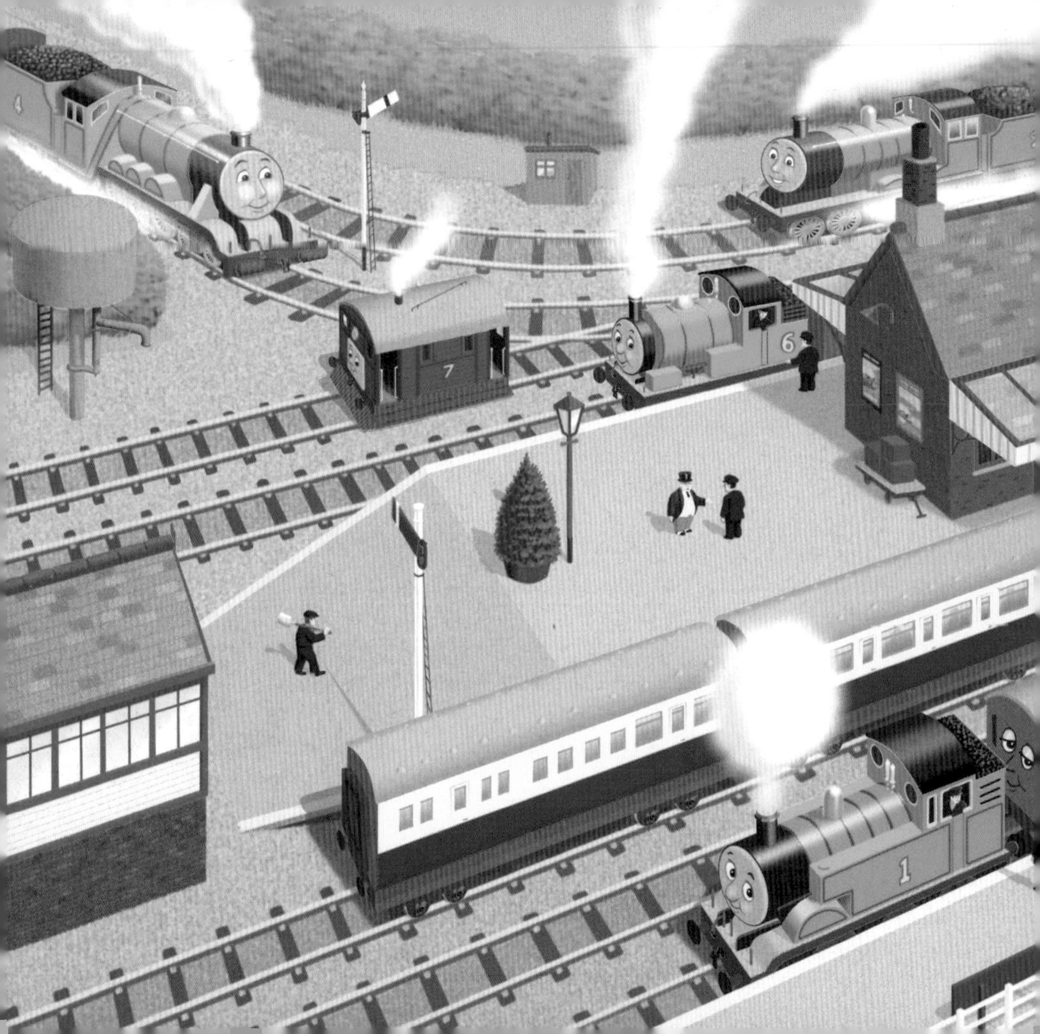
4
7
6
1

The Thomas Story Library is THE definitive collection of stories about Thomas and ALL his Friends.

5 more Thomas Story Library titles will be chuffing into your local bookshop in April 2007:

Arthur
Caroline
Murdoch
Neville
Freddie

And there are even more Thomas Story Library books to follow later!

So go on, start your Thomas Story Library NOW!

A Fantastic Offer for Thomas the Tank Engine Fans!

STICK POUND COIN HERE

In every Thomas Story Library book like this one, you will find a special token. Collect 6 Thomas tokens and we will send you a brilliant Thomas poster, and a double-sided bedroom door hanger! Simply tape a £1 coin in the space above, and fill out the form overleaf.

TO BE COMPLETED BY AN ADULT

To apply for this great offer, ask an adult to complete the coupon below and send it with a pound coin and 6 tokens, to:
THOMAS OFFERS, PO BOX 715, HORSHAM RH12 5WG

☐ Please send a Thomas poster and door hanger. I enclose 6 tokens plus a £1 coin. (Price includes P&P)

Fan's name..

Address..

....Postcode..................................

Date of birth..

Name of parent/guardian..

Signature of parent/guardian...

Please allow 28 days for delivery. Offer is only available while stocks last. We reserve the right to change the terms of this offer at any time and we offer a 14 day money back guarantee. This does not affect your statutory rights.

☐ Data Protection Act: If you do not wish to receive other similar offers from us or companies we recommend, please tick this box. Offers apply to UK only.